Big Otis, Miss May and the OK Corral Bar-b-q

Patsy Stanley

ISBN -979-8-9879950-3-7

LCCN -2024913785

Chapter One

Blackberry Tarts an' lemon zingers
What we gonna' do wid' 'dem?
I say we turn 'em all into gun slingers
waitin' on a dock in da' bay!
Yep. Waitin' fer' trubble'
to sail on in heah'
Dat's what.

The blue eyed, sharp faced, middle aged woman from the southern mountain backwoods picked the wild blackberries the city folks never bothered with. A wordy, shy, homespun older woman with a rootless survival history no stranger ever asked about, Miss May lived her lonely, poverty ridden life determined to make the most of any resources that came to hand. In the unfamiliar environment of the big city, she stayed grimly and defiantly on target, just as she had in the many other places she'd lived.

She picked the blackberries growing along the streets of the city, her back turned to passersby, her fingers nimbly plucking the dark, plump berries off their thorny vines, carefully easing them into containers while shouldering back the mean, thorny vines the fat, purple berries hung from.

"Humph!" Miss May muttered as she picked.

Busy pedestrians stopped to stare at her endeavors before they politely shook their heads and hastily moved on. They had better things to do than to watch an old country woman full of odd notions picking the neglected blackberries patches that grew everywhere in the city.

Embarrassed, shy and forever angry, but full of common sense that dictated no waste be allowed with nature's bounty, Miss May muttered defiantly at them.

"Damn fool people here never even look at them shiny, purple, fat blackberries jist' a' hangin', waitin' fer' somebody to pick 'em an' put 'em to good use! Don't cost a thing!"

Blackberries grew everywhere in the big, bustling, people-washed, rainy city she'd somehow landed in far away from the mountain home she'd started out in.

When everything she'd brought was full, she rushed the bursting, ripe berries home to her little shacky place as fast as she could. For the sake of economy and to save time, she always took Green Street. Her hips and knees liked going downhill a whole lot better than going uphill.

Back home, she rushed the berries quick and careful to the sink in the tiny kitchen before they squashed each other into slamback, mulled up, mushy juice, fit only fer' wine makin'. She didn't drink wine. Nor imbibe in that damn white lightnin', neither. An' she wouldn't go to jail fer' bootleggin' it, either, like her kin back home. Shame on em'!

She gentled the fragile berries into the sink, then grabbed the worn tart pans from the rack above the stove. They'd been hopeful and shiny way back when. She didn't want to think of how long ago way back when was.

She surged forward with the job at hand, humming as she tenderly sorted, rinsed and baked the fragile, juicy blackberries into the fine tasting tarts she sold to Big Otis up at the OK Corral Bar-b-q.

It seemed that Miss May had found a way to carve out a tiny niche for herself with her delicious tarts, even if they carried just a hint of bitterness along with their sweetness.

"Hav' ta' do sumthin'," she muttered with a frown of satisfaction.

"Sumthin' ta' make a buck."

As she worked, in her mind she compared the city blackberries to the blackberries growing wild on the hillsides of her mountain home. Back home, the berries were smaller and tarter. She snorted.

"That's 'cause it never stops rainin' here."

Memories, both good and bad, deepened the silence she worked in, adding unseen hints of her character, warm red courage, and the resilience of a confused lifetime to the flavor of each tart. Loneliness, poverty, and the challenges of aging would not stop Miss May from the simple pleasure of creating something sweet and good with her hands.

But ever' once in a while, when she'd gone beyond mad, she made thumb-sized lemon tarts, maybe a million of 'em. How many depended on how far past mad she'd gone.

She called 'em lemon zingers, and made 'em deadly tart and beyond sweet until they tasted 'zactly like the ninety eight degrees of hell between bad choices, old unfairness and loneliness she suffered from daily.

Today, she made one pan full, jist' to keep her hand in, to remind her of the daily task of not losing her temper and needing to allus' have the last word.

She hummed to herself while she worked, the lemon tarts reflecting her mood. Even though she had trapped herself in this big city, she took pride in her baking and her ability to survive and even thrive in any circumstances.

Big Otis's customers swore Miss May's lemon tarts would kill 'em — at least give 'em ulcers — but they come back for more ever' time. She knew why they come back, but didn't say nuthin'.

She made 'em 'cause she knowed she didn't have a chance of a snowball in hell of gittin' outta' this big, soppin' wet city where ever' thing smelt like fish or mold. A cold and unforgiving city, where she watched the wealthy and well connected get cared for. Everybody else was on their own. Well, she was on her own. And, too old now to make another getaway. That startin' gate had closed.

"I got no car. An' only skinny livin' money."

She charged four dolla' twenty cents a haf' dozen for the regular size blackberry tarts. Four dolla' twenty cents a haf' dozen for the tiny shriekin' lemon tarts, 'cause the juice ain't free. Nor the flour. Nor the shortenin'. Nor the electric.

When she was done, she straightened her back and dusted her hands. Then she straightened the tiny, cracked mirror hanging on its nail on the wall and peered into it.

Yes, her hair was all white now, not dusty blond any more. No salt and pepper hair like Big Otis. Big Otis said his hair was once an admirable dark brown. Matched his pretty ebony eyes and skin, he said, laughing. Or at least the ladies swore it to him back in the day.

The two of them had much in common. They didn't need to use words about some things. That was a relief. The past they never spoke of was plumb full of shouting, justified hurt and red faced, dust eatin' shame. No need to ever go over none of that damn ol' pacin', mumblin' misery agin'.

Miss May grinned to herself in the mirror. They'd both been through hell. They understood that about each other. Oh, it was different kinds of hell, but hell was still hell, anyway you cut it.

They shared a common bond forged by their past experiences and struggles.

They didn't always see eye to eye, but their deep affection for each other kept them respectful of each other's ways. Mainly they shared an unwavering commitment to doing what was right, especially for those less fortunate. She turned away from the mirror and began washing bowls and big spoons.

The tarts were done and cooled off by late afternoon. They smelled hopeful and sweet in her little home. She sucked in their aroma and grinned, memories of mountains and Nature's good bounty feeding her lonely soul.

Chapter Two

It ain't right, but it keeps on going up anyways.
    High rise 'partments.
    High rise flour
    High rise bakin' powder
    Ain't no place else ta' git' good biscuits

Miss May packed up the tarts. Slid them into a worn brown grocery sack. Then she changed into her good slacks and a pullover top. She slipped her feet into her worn sneakers and tied them and set out on her journey. She had to carry the tarts three blocks. All uphill. Comin' home, it would be down, down, downhill. Almost runnin' over herself on the way home. Up or down, it was still a hell of a task.

"It's either all uphill or all downhill in this dam' big ol' wet city!" she grumbled.

"Ain't nothin' free 'round here 'cept them damn blackberries," she grumbled.

Miss May was one who saw past the façade of "progress" to the heart of the matter. The matter was the displacement of old people because of the steady, ongoing loss of community. Kids and nobody else wanted to deal with the discomfort, pain, and ugliness of aging. Yep. The haves and the have nots were still in business. Maybe she was wrong. Maybe she was right. But that was her thinkin' on it.

Miss May's leg muscles were getting tight due to her uphill climb. They might wear out. She hoped it wasn't soon. If they did, she'd do what she allus' did. Set down on the cee-ment curb and wait until her legs were able to go again. Wasn't nothing new in it. No other choice. She'd had to stop before. Too many times.

"Dam' hills in 'dis town!" she muttered to herself again.

She stopped to catch her breath when she was almost there. Sat down on the curb.

"Gotta' slow down. Doan' wanna' seem hasty. Eager'll git ya' nothin' in dis' town." she thought grimly.

She rested and watched Big Otis strolled down the sidewalk towards the pharmacy on the corner like he never had a care in the world, nor nothing else to do but lollygag around.

Big Otis stopped in front of the pharmacy. He started talkin' mournful-like to the skinny little ol' man weavin' back and forth in front of the pharmacy doors. The little ol' thing was holdin' onto his cheap walker for dear life. That same little ol' man couldn't hardly walk. She knew, 'cause she'd seen him before in the same predicament.
She watched him wet his pants while he stood there, swayin' back and forth. She watched the dark stain spread across the front of his tan, worn pants. He bowed his head in

shame and started weeping at what he'd done again.

Miss May dropped her eyes to the sidewalk, searching for something to do or say. She wanted to help, needed to, but couldn't think of anything right quick. Anger rose in her.

The city stayed carefully and legally indifferent towards the struggles of its elderly citizens. The bustling city people passing by and into the busy pharmacy courteously ignored the old man's plight.

That little ol' man lived at the other end of the block in the ugly gray high rise the city had built a few months ago. Cheap senior living, the city called it. Storage bins for useless old folks. Then the city built a giant pharmacy on the other end of the block. Big Otis's Bar-b-q stood halfway between them.

With hot eyes, Miss May glanced uphill at the ugly high rise loomin' on the corner and shivered.

That ol' man didn't have nobody. He was jist' tryin' to make it to the pharmacy down the hill a block from his livin' quarters to get the meds to keep him quiet.

Nobody helped him 'cause he had no money or big shot name to give 'em. No moolah. Green stuff. Cash. Bucks. She sniffed. He only got skinny money, jist' like her.

She stared down at the cracked and crumbling sidewalk until she calmed down. Her sense of righteousness was tempered by practical self-wisdom. There was only so much she could do to help in a world stacked against her. She had to watch her blood pressure.

Chapter Three

A Georgia Peach
from south Atlanta
his ribs tastin' like angel food
pleasin' the customers
at the OK Corral Bar-b-q

Her thoughts flew to Big Otis. Now, there was a man she could count on! Big Otis and her agreed on most ever' thing. A big giant who owned a soul sweet like honey. A good man. A fine brother.

Big Otis come from Atlanta, Georgia. He was a backwoods Georgia peach. He wasn't the sweet little clingy peach kind, though. That's 'cause he come from tough assed backwoods folks. Big Otis had boxed his way to freedom by beatin' up and gittin' beat up long enough to make the dough, the bread, the moolah to buy his little shack of a house and start his bar-b-q place in it.

He'd bought the little white clapboard house when Third Street was thin. Now his house was the only one left on Third Street. He'd bought it awhile before the city built the high rise on the upper corner from him, before they added a giant, fancy, two-story pharmacy down on the other corner from him.

Then the city widened the street way past puttin' up with. Two lanes each way and a turn lane in the middle. Took a half hour to git' across it!

Big Otis and Miss May did for each other. Whatever was needed. Their relationship was steeped in a mix of understanding, banter, with both avoiding the unspoken past. Despite their many differences, despite the odds stacked against them, they found ways to stay united in the fight to do what was right, to be good hearted to others.

Miss May sighed and stood. She picked up the bag of tarts and carried it on up to Big Otis' place. She stood on the sidewalk and glanced down, expectin' to see just busted cee-ment, but two dandelions had blasted their way through a crack in the cee-ment.

"Hmpph!" she muttered to herself, admiring the tough assed, carefree dandelions, yellow and bold, caressing them with her eyes.

The makeshift dining area outside Big Otis's Bar-b-q joint, with its resilient, mismatched tables, tarps and faded memories, stubbornly refused to be swept aside by progress.

She'd asked him why he named it the OK Corral Bar-b-q. He said he liked old westerns. And old folks. And helpin' people. The OK Corral was a disguised sanctuary, he'd said. Rollin' his eyes heavenward. She'd snorted. But he'd stuck to his guns.

She set the bag down on a round, plastic patio table. Miss May's presence there, with her tarts and her quiet defiance was a testament to the rest of the enduring spirits living in the city. They lived hard and alone, but they knew they had each other.

She looked around. The city kept tryin' to persuade Big Otis to sell his place. A big shot dropped by ever' little while an' offered him a bucket a' money for the place, but he wouldn't sell.

Miss May's mind darted back to the little old man. She stuck out her sharp chin. Hot, righteous anger rose in her again on behalf of him. She let the anger swell. That little ol' man couldn't git' mad anymore. Mad had been wrung out of him by fear and years, so she'd damn well do it for him.

She squinted... Though she was sort of getting' close behind in age. Sort of. Maybe. She didn't like to think about it. Her mind left that subject alone.

Her and Big Otis could never see the use of doin' such silly, mean things as makin' ol' people live up in the sky. Stacked up there in tiny boxes when anybody worth their salt knowed that ol' folks should be grounded to the Earth, so they could go on understandin' impendin' matters with Nature as their teacher.
Big Otis and her shook their heads together in sorrow at the folly of life sometimes. But the

big city said it had no room to spare, and everything kept buildin' up higher. Higher and higher. It ain't right, but it keeps on goin' up anyways, she thought grimly.

Miss May watched Big Otis stomp back up the hill an' quick set out a cheap, white, plastic chair on the sidewalk outside his patio, reserved fer' fine dinin'.

He set the chair out past the two long, pink leather Caddy seats restin' on the cee-ment patio beneath a canvas tarp tacked to four tall posts. The seats had been confiscated from the empty shell of the Cadillac shell parked out back, a memento of his Georgia boxing days.

"Cadillac Man" had been his boxing name. Whuppin' ass had been his game.

A faded photo of the long-as-a-small-train Caddy hung on a rusty nail, proudly crooked on the wall, right above the eating table in the tiny dining room of the linoleum floored and back doored little old wood house.

Outside that back door rested the empty Caddy shell. It sat up on blocks in the weedy strip of dirt filled with busted up cee-ment, where more yellow dandelions bloomed like hell or maybe heaven.

The Caddy shell kept steadily rustin' in the fine rain that fell on ever' thing in the big city ever' day, washing the city down like a young one getting washed down ever' night before it

was put to bed. Yep. That was Big Otis'
backyard.

Miss May cocked her head sideways as she
watched Big Otis stride back down the sidewalk
towards the pharmacy. She grinned as people
stepped aside. She could tell he meant business.
She guessed they did, too! Lawdy! Nobody got in
that big boxer's way!

She watched Big Otis sweep up the weeping,
white haired little ol' man in one arm and grab
his walker in his other big ham fist.

Big Otis carried the ol' man up the street in
his arms like the little ol' thing was jist' a itty'
bitty' baby, leanin' over him like the ol' man was
a feather that might escape his big, muscled
arms any minute.

Big Otis toted the pissy little featherweight up
the hill and settled him down real easy into the
plastic chair. He parked the ol' man's walker
beside the chair, went inside and come back out
holding a handful of paper towels.

He laid 'em on the ol' man's lap. The old man
stopped cryin' and wiped the crotch of his pants
with the paper towels. Big Otis grabbed the
soiled towels when he was done and stomped
over to the green plastic garbage can.

Big Otis threw the paper towels in the
garbage can with a big smile, not makin' a bad
face, for the little ol' man was watching him.
He went inside and brought out a pan of soapy
water and a dish towel, leaned over an'

washed the old man's pissy hands. He tossed the water on the dandelions growing in the cee-ment and took the pan and towel inside.

He came back out and laid another stack of paper towels on the old man's lap and set a plate with one rib on the towels. No pinto beans, no collard greens, no corn, just a rib an' a slice of heavily buttered light bread.

Miss May stared at the light bread and shook her head mournfully. Too much butter. But she understood why he overdid it. He was a man. It was sad that such a great big man didn't know that hot, purty yellow cornbread went best with ribs. Men. She shook her head in despair.

She avoided his glance, studying the patio tables instead. "Property of Ellsworth Calhoun," they read, on the sides of the biggest round white tables.

She'd already asked Big Otis who that was a bunch a' times. He told her a different story ever' time she asked. She figured Ellsworth Calhoun was some kind of big-time party man. The main story Big Otis told her was that he'd found them tables alongside a road somewhere. That one might be true.

Miss May put her hands on her hips and studied Big Otis each time he told her one of his big, fishy yarns. He allus' waited, grinnin'.

"You's lyin'," she'd finally declare.

Big Otis allus' answered, "Stop askin' so many questions, then."

She'd nod and grin up at him.

"Your bidness," she'd finally say, allus' needin' to have the last word, shrugging.

"I needs to have the last word."

Big Otis always nodded and turned away.

"That's the truth if God ever told it." he'd mutter and roll his eyes up towards Heaven every time. She knowed he did that, 'cause she'd watched him plenty of times.

Chapter Four

High rises an' high prices
Big city blues
cold sidewalks
an' colder voices
ain't welcomin' you!

Miss May waited until Big Otis disappeared back inside before she opened the brown grocery bag holding the tart pans. She gently pulled out a tart pan. With her little pinkie stuck out, sneakers untied again, she looked the lemon zingers over, eyes squinted.

She plucked out a particular lemon zinger. Then she delicately placed it beside the rib on the ol' man's plate like she was servin' the most important ol' man that ever lived upon this Earth. Maybe Moses or his granddaddy Methusala, who died at 969 years of age. Maybe it would offer him some comfort.

Maybe the ol' man needed the cleansing anger strength that particular lemon zinger jist' might bring to him. Strengthen his stomach and maybe his bladder, too, if it didn't kill him. That's what she was thinkin'.

Big Otis came back out and stood there, watchin' her, sweatin' hard like he'd jist' been in a knockout boxin' match again. Miss May stared at him. Navigating the complexities of their friendship and this town put a lot on her mind sometimes.

"What the hell's the matter with you?" she asked.

"What you sweatin' fo'?"

He rolled his eyes heavenward.

"My Mama and Daddy back home in Atlanta learnt' me ta' respect and take care of ol' folks. They said they be watchin' me close from the grave, an' if I didn't do it right, they said they'd come straight out of their graves an' stomp my sorry ass inta' the ground!"

Wiping the sweat off his face, he trembled like a little sissy. He looked around to see if any of the Unseens were visitin'.

Then he went back inside an' brought out a cold bottle of root beer with a straw sticking out of it. The old man reached out and grabbed the drink in a grateful, shaky hand, almost dropped it, then steadied it.

She watched as the lonesome, skinny straw made its slow way up to his mouth. It took a roundabout route and a couple of short detours. He finally grabbed the straw in his mouth and sucked on it noisily, like a baby does a bottle when its mama ain't holdin' the bottle right, so they don't get air in their stomach and start a bellyache.

She studied the ol' man. Big Otis and her had the strength and resilience of those who refuse to be broken by their circumstances. So far. The ol' man didn't. His resistance was gone. Probably long ago. The ol' man needed the root beer.

The inevitable fine, slow misty rain began to fall. Nothing new in that. The misty rain served as a backdrop to their conversation, cleansing and renewing all three of them.

"Wonder why the rain doesn't wash away this city's wrongdoing?" she said softly.

"Too many humans here." Big Otis answered softly.

Miss May gusted out a long suffering breath and stood, leavin' the little pissy ol' man to chaw on his rib bone and suck on his straw. She picked up the bag of tarts and carried them inside. She placed them on the brown, round wood table in the dining room. Once a living room, it was the largest room in the house.

The wood table was ugly, cheap, overworked, and odd looking with loopy scrolls and curves hiding beneath its top.

She asked Big Otis every so often, where the fancy wood table come from. He gave her different answers. He said the fancy table was from a fancy dining room in a fancy hotel. But she never believed that story, either.

She cocked her head and went back outside and stood in his patio dinin' room. That's what he called it. It ran across the front part of his place and out to the sidewalk. A cee-ment square with log fencing two feet high around the front of it. The plastic covered pink Caddy seats set facin' each other in the middle of the patio. White plastic tables and unmatched chairs set here and there.

Miss May glanced up at the large, hand printed black and white sign nailed above the front door of the little white wood house.

"Big Otis's OK Corral Bar-b-q."

She watched Big Otis come out and wrestle the wood under the bar-b-q grill in the corner. She measured his wide shoulders with her eyes while he bent over the grill.

The smoke rose up from the fresh wood and made him cough. She frowned. Big Otis said his folks was Louisiana swamp people who knowed the ins and outs and ways of mean ghosts.

He said his father got con-scripted into the Army and was sent to Atlanta and never did leave there. There was a lot more to his story, but she could never git' more of it outta' him.

She tapped her foot, then clapped her hands on her hips. Well, maybe his folks knowed sumpthin' 'bout them matters, an' jist' maybe they didn't. Maybe she shouldn't believe that story either.

But the goodness of him always stuck in her craw or soul — somewhere, anyways.

She sighed before she glared at him and announced loudly, "That'll be ten dollas' and seventy fo' cents!"

Big Otis nodded and went inside to get the money. She followed him inside, little behind his back and likin' it. He was the biggest man she'd ever met. Over six foot five, somewhere in there. Great big heavy bones, body wide as a boxcar, with a solid bunch of muscle weight. All muscle, she thought, picturin' him boxing and killin' off all a' her damn enemies fer' her while she turned a wood crate upside down, set down on it, an' watched him as he killed off her enemies alive and dead and some that never broke bread with anyone else, jist' theirselves.

Big Otis glanced back at her.

She watched him admiringly, and he let her alone until her soul calmed down again.

"Best make some more tarts and braing' 'em in on Wednesday if ya' can. An' can ya' go out and set with the ol' man a little bit?"

He asked her these things in his hollow, full of old times mournful voice, in his ancient, big boomin' bell of a hollow voice, while he wiped the tabletop down with a large, damp rag.
The smell of bleach floated up to her nose. She sneezed, turned away, and wandered back outside without answering him, his deep, resonant tone echoing in her ears and heart. She

sighed. Big Otis could be melancholy, too. A shared, unspoken moment of nostalgia and sadness.

"Cain't fix nothin' much." Acceptance of that fact.

She looked down at the ol' man. He looked jist' as done in as she felt after climbing them three dam' blocks ta' get here.

He nodded in and out of sleep over his one rib. The rib was barely gnawed on. She nodded with satisfaction 'cause the lemon zinger was gone.

She grabbed a white plastic chair and pulled it up close, facin' the ol' man, like she was talkin' to him. She settled down into the chair, stretched out a bit, and nodded off, resentful that it was Big Otis' fault that she allus' fell asleep when she did bidness' with his bar-b-q joint, but she 'allus gave in, fer' it was the best damn sleep she ever got!

Chapter Five

Sleepin' habits and workin' habits
worn down to blue
by both him and her
and yes, by maybe you too

Miss May woke up to find Big Otis looming over her. The other white plastic chair was empty. She peered up at Big Otis.

"Where's the ol' man?" Big Otis beamed his wide grin down on her.

"Carried him back up to his place, on up to the third floor, opened his box, put him in his crib bed, and pulled up the covers," he announced smugly, still grinning at her.

"I set his medicine on his nightstand."

He jerked one large thumb towards the top of the hill where the tall concrete box dotted with tiny windows here and there, loomed over everything in the vicinity like a lofty, ugly omen of bad times to come. She followed his look.

"They's people who lives in apartments they whole lives, don't git' treated like that."

Miss May studied Big Otis and nodded slowly.

"Wish I had somebody to help me out like you helps him," she answered in a voice heavy with both resentment and hope.

"I lives in a ramshackle little ol' place," she whined, lookin' up at him with small, piercing blue eyes under eyebrows like the wings of a moth or maybe a blue jay, eyes that he'd seen widen a time or two into blazing blue fire, the kind of fire only seen on a red hot day at high noon, when Miss May come across somethin' she didn't like or something that upset her.

Big Otis stared down at the little woman splashed into the cheap plastic chair like a pear shaped puddle, yella' hair turned all white, wrinkles around her eyes, mouth and chin. Her bony hands lay restless in her lap like they was ashamed not to be workin'. Her stubborn little mouth curved was curved down in a bow under her sharp little nose.

He shook his head. Miss May didn't want his help. Or need it. She was jist rattlin' on. He suspected she did that 'cause nobody ever give her much attention back in her early days.

He wiped his face with a big hand. Mist fell every day in the big city. The mist showered the big city relentlessly until seven every night when the city lights came on, drivin' the rollin' fog and the fine rain back out to sea. Next morning, the mist was back.

Big Otis and Miss May held their faces up to the mist. The mist was soft, and cooled Miss May's hot mind. She wondered why the cleansing mist never cleaned up the city's bad ways. Especially the serial killers she'd read about who used the mystery of rain to cover up their vile deeds.

Big Otis thought of damp earth and gravestones every morning when the mist began. It made him mournful and sadder than he wanted to be. The mist seemed to know this. It gentled itself into the creases on his face and dampened his hair and shirt collar. The Unseens were checkin' up on him agin', he guessed.

"I cain't do nothin' much for ya'."

Miss May swung her stare up towards him, then dropped her eyes, accepting his words. She sighed. It's a thing she's asked before, too many times. She knows it. He knows it. He wasn't the right one to ask. Somebody was, but not him. He knows it. She knows it. They both knew it wasn't money she was asking him for.

"Just keepin' in practice." she said.

"I know." he answered. "Go ahead."

A long, silent time passed, Miss May said, "Well, gimme' two a' them ribs an' dock my pay fer' 'em from the next tart order."

They both sighed with relief. Big Otis nodded and turned to go back inside. She stared at his broad back. It looked like it was about an acre across. Somebody would have to walk a half hour to git' across it. He was so big he shoulda' been ponderous, but he wasn't.

"I'm light on my feet, but not from bein' gray headed." he told her smartly on a long, gray day when he'd worn a troubled, mournful look all day long. Because of it, she'd accused him of not being ponderous enough.

"Comes from boxin' when I was young. Otherwise, I mighta' been jist' a heap of dead wood."

"You's gray headed." She'd peered up at him, looking him up and down judiciously.

"You's white headed," he'd retorted, lookin' down at her, eyes swelled big with unspoken misery.

"And you's big. An' middle aged or more," she'd responded.

"And you's little. At least compared to me. An' I ain't guessin' your age. But you ain't no spring chicken, dat's fo' sure!" Big Otis answered. Miss May studied him a minute. His eyes were smilin' now. She never said no more.

She took the ribs and went home to eat and nap. Restless when she woke up, she looked in the cupboard and remembered the canned peaches from the food bank.

After some deliberation, she decided to make peach tarts. She returned to Big Otis's place a few hours later carrying a large batch of the peach tarts. Little did she know that this innocent act was the beginning of something new. That the peach tarts would set off a chain of unexpected changes in her life.

Miss May would find herself pulled into an unexpected adventure, one that started with the simple act of baking that would change her life in ways she never could have imagined.

Chapter Six

Ribs and bosses, collards and beans
make ya' fat and happy and
sometimes sassy
and mean
til' trubble walks in…
Here's where…
Trouble walked right into the OK Corral bar-b-q.

Here's what Trouble with a capital T looked like. A man. Fairly tall. Smooth. Handsome. An alluring, natural presence, a blend of masculinity and wise, learned tenderness. Golden tan skin and exotic eyes hinted at a tropical or islander background. The man moved as if creating music with every step. The rhythm of his island was in his feet.

He was, as is usual for women of all ages in this old weary world, Man Trouble. Miss May would soon find out that she was not exempt from the hope and passion she took for granted, had died in her long ago. Well, it wasn't dead, and it might make her mind it again.

Shortly before Mr. Trouble with a capital T strolled through the door, Miss May held out a pan of peach tarts for Big Otis to look over.

"These peach tarts are free today. Not tomorrow, though. These are tasters. If you like 'em, I'll add 'em to my available menu of see-lect desserts."

She chose a tart, grabbed one of Big Otis'
giant paws, turned it over, and set the tart
gently on his palm.

"Go on, taste test it."

Big Otis popped the tart into his mouth and
chewed. A big smile wreathed his face. But
before he could speak, she fixed her gaze on the
worn linoleum floor under her feet.

Mournfully, she admitted, "Them peaches
didn't grow wild here. They's canned peaches."
She glared up at him defensively. "They's all I
had to work with."

Big Otis wasn't listening. He was chewing,
looking past her. A client had just strolled in.
Miss May turned around. As the man danced
lightly into the OK Corral Bar-b-q,-best ribs in
the city!- Big Otis and Miss May's eyes looked
him over. He was about Miss May's age, with
short gray hair. He was dressed in some sort of
spiffy uniform. Trouble had a way of making a
grand entrance sometimes!

They watched the man cross the room. With
each step, he seemed to weave a melody in the
air, a symphony of allure that left Miss May
suddenly spellbound. Caught off guard, Miss
May, well, she found herself caught up in the
spell, unable to tear her gaze away from Trouble
with a capital T.
Miss May felt drawn to the man, like a moth to a
flame. His aura exuded magnetism, a potent mix
of charm and mystery that left her

breathless, unable to resist the gravitational pull of his presence.

"Can I help you, sir?" Big Otis asked while Miss May stood there in frozen wonder, gaping at the stranger.

The man advanced on them. There was music in the way he strolled across the room towards them, smiling his wide smile.

"Yes. My boss sent me to purchase ribs. He's waiting outside in the car. He would like a sample rib, if possible, and may I try one of the peach tarts you were just speaking of?"

Open mouthed, Miss May picked up a peach tart and handed it to the man. He popped it into his mouth and chewed while they waited. A look of delight spread over his face.

"Delicious! Why, these beat anything my boss's chef makes," the man said. "How many do you have available?"

She picked up the full tart pans and placed them in Big Otis's hands.

"I made 'em. But they's his. We ain't even took 'em out of the pans yet'."

"I'd like to purchase all of them. Can you show me any more wares you might have available?" the man asked politely.

Miss May stared down at the large, worn down to the wood patch in the linoleum.

"I used canned peaches," she confessed sullenly to both Big Otis and the stranger.

The man stared at her.

"Does that make a difference? I don't know the first thing about cooking, nor does my boss. He's an expert in other things. I just know this is delicious."

Miss May and Big Otis stared at the man. He stared back, waiting. Finally, he broke the silence.

"Do you mind if I try another?"

They watched as he reached out, almost involuntarily, and snatched up another peach tart and popped it in his mouth.

'Mmm...heavenly," he said, wiping imaginary crumbs from his mouth.

He reached for a third peach tart, and she grabbed the pans and backed up.

"That's all the sample you get!" she said sharply, feeling her cheeks start to burn. Why, she hadn't blushed since she didn't remember when!

"Pardon me!" the man said, blushing himself.

"It's okay." she finally drawled, glancing at him and blushing red as a beet again.

Big Otis stared at the two of them. Back and forth. Then understanding dawned on him. They liked each other! He could feel the chemistry between them!

The white haired mouthy little puddle of a woman who cooked like Jesus was sittin' at the table, and the gray-haired, stocky, darkly tanned, muscled man in his chauffer's uniform staring back at him. How about that?

Big Otis watched the blue fire he remembered start a slow kindle in Miss May's eyes. He studied the man a minute. Pity for him warred with curiosity. Poor guy.

"You're pretty muscled up there. You been a boxer?" he asked the man hopefully.

"No, sir. But I was a football player back in my younger days."

He hesitated. "I must get back to my boss."

"Jist' a minute then," Big Otis said. Neither one of them answered him. No yes. No no. They just kept starin' at each other.

Big Otis fast-stepped into the kitchen. Chuckling, he quickly ripped off foil and wrapped a rack of ribs in it. He looked around for his special Tupperware containers to put the peach tarts in. He'd pack em' in there so's the man would have an excuse to return them, otherwise them two wouldn't have any reason to see each other agin'. He grinned. A man had to be quick on his toes if he was gonna' be a damn good matchmaker.

He grabbed his best Tupperware and carried the foiled ribs and empty Tupperware out of the tiny, steamy kitchen into the not much bigger dining room.

That's why I keeps' them Caddy' seats out front under that rain tarp, he thought proudly. Days like this. Yeah. Days like this!

He laid the ribs down on the table and began filling the Tupperware containers with peach tarts.

The little dinin' room was crackling with energy from the two silent lovebirds, clueless as to who each other was. Miss May looked ten years younger; the ex-football man's chest looked even broader. There was a manly flush on his face.

Well, that's that. Big Otis thought. Wonder what's next?

He fished under the table and came out with a worn, brown paper grocery bag. He carefully stacked the ribs and tarts in it.

"That'll be thirty five dollars and fifty cents," he said, dusting his big hands together.

The chauffer nodded but didn't answer. He reached in his back pocket and took out his wallet with a strong, well-shaped hand.

"Here's two twenties," he said. "Keep the change."

"Okay. I'll put it toward what she still owes me for all them ribs she keeps takin' home."

Big Otis meant it as joke. He and Miss May grinned at each other and snickered. But the chauffer scowled and took out his wallet again.

"I don't want this little lady owing anybody, so here."

He tossed a hundred-dollar bill on the tabletop, picked up the grocery bag, walked to the door, and stopped.

With his back to them, he said, "I'll be back Wednesday to purchase whatever wares you may have available, and at that time, I would request that you tell me your name, little tart lady."

The two of them stared at the back of the man's neck. It was red as a penalty flag thrown in the Super Bowl.

Miss May had rid herself of Man Trouble a long time ago, but she still had plenty in her left to say. And, she'd allus' got the last word in with them. That wasn't going to change. Or was it?

Miss May started to speak, but Big Otis nudged her, almost knocking her over. She staggered and grabbed the table.

"Hush up, girl!" he whispered. Out loud he bellowed at the man's back, "We'll see ya' next Wednesday."

She stared at the empty doorway, her mouth open. Big Otis knew she needed to have the last word, and she didn't git' it this time.

"Well, Halleluah fer' once!"

Big Otis muttered as he folded up the hundred dollar bill and shoved it into her hands. She examined it to make sure it was real. Then she shoved it deep into her pocket. She looked up at Big Otis.

"Well, I'll be. Now what?"

Big Otis gave her a knowing grin. She stared down at the floor, red-faced. Big Otis put his hands on his hips and smirked.

"Looks like you're in bidness', definitely in the tart bidness', and now, maybe in a little bit of monkey bidness', too!"

With the promise of future business and a potential romantic connection in the offing, Miss May and Big Otis found themselves facing a new chapter of unexpected events and possibilities. He laughed, shook his head, and moseyed back into the kitchen. She followed him.

"Need help fillin' them call-in orders? I can pack up the pintos and collard greens. I got time." she said to his broad back.

"Go right ahead," Big Otis answered, leanin' over and sniffing the kettle of beans.

"They's plumb ready."

He turned off the burner, where they had been simmerin' on low.

Behind him, Miss May grabbed a stack of the cheap paper bowls he'd ordered from a hotel job he'd held back in Atlanta before he went to boxin', and went to fillin' the orders.

"Gotta' clear my mind!"

Miss May muttered to herself. She kept on talkin' to herself. Big Otis grinned and acted like he couldn't hear a word she said.

As they work together in the kitchen, they each contemplated the implications of this unexpected turn of events, leaving them both

curious and a little fearful of what the future
might hold. All kinds of possibilities lay before
them now.

36

Chapter Seven

Wails and Woes and fancy clothes
Mornin's filled with sneezin'
So open yer' winda's
an' heft yer' gizzies
cause fer' some,
there jist' ain't no pleasin'

Miss May's routine was as predictable as the morning sun coming up. She snapped awake and lay still as a stone while her mind filled to the damn brim with misery. Thoughts of aging, of pain, of more miseries, and most of all, of aloneness. The misery loomed large, casting shadows that threatened to swallow her whole, like that damn whale had done to Jonah.

But she fought back- by sneezing. Miss May got busy takin' her regular mornin' sneezin' fits. She'd heard long ago back home, that every sneeze cast a demon thought out of ya'.

Well, she was filled to the brim every morning with them little demon brats! The sneezin' fits raced in ever' morning to run off the damn demon thinking.

Miss May refused to ever give in entirely to that damn morning despair, but sometimes she needed to sleep in a little bit longer.
When the morning sneezing fits finally left, she opened her window. She welcomed the cool,

damp air that filled her room. A misty rain fell all day, most every day in a steady rhythm that moisturized her face and made it easier to practice smiling, something she wasn't good at. She decided to go blackberry picking, rain be damned.

Back home, they had four seasons. Not jist' one long, wet year round rainy season like here in this big city.

Back in childhood days, she'd collected weeks of Redemption after a fallin; out, stayin' away, hidin' out, fer' she made pies and cobblers her family couldn't fault, and she canned fruit jars full a' berries, an' they left her alone to do it so's they could eat it all up in the winter.

Those days, she was a young 'un with no voice an' no one to listen to it anyways. She shoved the past away with the hip movement she'd practiced while watchin' roller derby on TV. Until they took it off. Said it was too damn violent. Huh!

She shoved her feet into her worn sneakers, bent over wearily and tied 'em. Then she grabbed her berry pickin' stuff and set out before she could talk herself out of it. That's the only way she got things done. If she waited one itty bitty minute to git' to somethin', her mind would go agin' her and it might be too late, an' she'd end up wanderin' around agin' like a damn hobo who didn't know what train to ketch.

Miss May was determined to find some small joy or solace in the midst of survival. She'd done it before, time and again. Mushrooms in the shaded, cool, woody hills back home. Sea shells that smelled like the calcium lick for their milk cows back home. Trillium blooming in the shaded, black, moist dirt in the spring. Wild sweet strawberries, tiny and hiding under vines and their leaves, peeking out at her red and waiting to be picked.

Miss May made her way to the familiar, overgrown blackberry thicket hidden in the back of an old field about a half mile from her place. She set her things down, slapped her hands on her hips and studied the thicket.

Each berry looked like a clump of tiny round skins, holding sacks of purple juice, each berry about a half a thumb long and round. The sacks of purple juice were clumped together in a bunch, hanging, just waiting to be picked. But it wasn't that easy, and Miss May knew it. the berries hung under protective thorn vines just itchin' to stab somebody.

She looked them over and made a plan of attack. Well, all her life, berry patches had kept her away from more meanness than she could count, and probably too much, if not more, of sin. She snickered. Humming to herself, she skillfully navigated the thorny vines, expertly picking the ripe berries, filling her containers to the brim.

The berry picking went fast. She headed back home, everything she could carry filled with ripe blackberries.

She was satisfied with her successful picking session, wasn't that enough? Miss May pushed away the hopeful, romantic thoughts about the peach-buyin' man she'd met, and tried to stay focused on the task at hand, which was baking fresh blackberry tarts in her tiny kitchen.

As she worked, she repeated her morning prayer, finding solace in its familiarity. And although her efforts to distract herself didn't always succeed, she remained determined to keep moving forward, one day at a time.

"Ain't no hell like thinkin' about a man," she complained to nobody there, shoving a pan of tarts into the oven. She deliberately remembered all she'd been through with men, ticking the memories off, trying to root out the hope that was slow blossomin' way down deep in her soul. She slammed around, and soon, fresh baked blackberry tarts were stacked all around, cooling off in the tiny kitchen. It was time to make thm damn lemon zingers again. She hoped makin' 'em would cool her off. Kill that new hope about that peach liking, purty, light footed, sun kissed, handsome, graceful, dark eyed, manly man. But sometimes hard labor worked. And sometimes it didn't. This time, it didn't. After three dozen lemon zingers, she quit trying.

Chapter Eight

Got dis' dam' big ol' cravin
got dis' dam' big 'ol yen
hopin' fer' dat' dam' big 'ol man's smile
cain't wait to lay eyes on him agin."

Miss May woke up early Wednesday morning, feeling the weight of the day ahead. Resentfully, she muttered her usual morning prayer for what little it would be worth this day.

"Damn men!' she muttered, stacking tart pans high, preparing for the trip to Big Otis's Bar-b-q. Carrying the load was taxing on her legs, but she knew it had to be done. She groaned. She'd have to make more than one trip today.

She trudged up the street in her worn sneakers, carrying the first load of tart pans tarts in a worn brown grocery sack.

A block from Big Otis' place, she sat down on the cee-ment curb and leaned back into the center of the tough, yellow dandelions growing in the grass strip between the curb and the sidewalk. They didn't give a care if anybody liked them being there or not. Miss May grinned at the dandelions.

She told them, "My Mama and Aunt Gizzon back home," she said, fending off the hot air pushin' over her from the traffic whizzin' by, "made yore' kind of magic, too. Why, they'd both perk right up after settin' in dandelions after a beat up of some kind."

She watched the dandelions grow brighter and tougher. She shook her head and grinned.

"Couldn't take the Light out of Mama and Aunt Gizzon or you'ns either! Ha ha!"

Miss May set there awhile, humming, taking solace by running her hands over the smooth yellow dandelion tops, sucking in their buttery cheer with her breath.

Cars whizzed by. A couple of them honked at her. She paid no attention. To hell with them. She stood up when she was ready, smoothed down the tunic that went best with her stretchy pants, picked up the tarts and moved on.

Up. Up. Up.

Arriving at Big Otis's Bar-b-q joint, she set the tarts on a patio table and sighed with relief. Then she realized she was much earlier than expected. She felt a pang of embarrassment at her miscalculation.

"Life must go on". She muttered to herself.

She picked up the bag and carried them inside. She carried the brown paper bag filled with tart pans over to the table and set them down on it.

"Whew!' she said, wiping her brow with one hand.

Big Otis stood there, towel in hand, watching her. Then he looked at the cheap, round clock with the faded white background and faded black hands hanging on a nail on the wall above the table.

Miss May followed his eyes.

"Yep. I'm too early."

Quickly conjuring up an excuse about needing to bring more tarts, Miss May defensively snapped the words at Big Otis, who chose not to challenge her. Wisely, he kept his mouth shut and just nodded.

She knew he knew better. She huffed out her breath and glared around, looking for something to slam. She'd slam a door, but there wasn't one nearby.

She turned and stormed out the door, head held high in unearned righteous indignation. Away from Big Otis's knowing eyes, she dropped her façade of anger.

Returning home to fetch the next batch of tarts, Miss May continued to mutter angrily about men and their ways.

"Dam' men!" she muttered. "They are allus' trying to make a woman lose her mind!"

Despite knowing that Big Otis didn't actually need her to sell her wares, she felt compelled to fulfill her commitment. She suspected Big Otis understood this. That's why he remained silent.

Chapter Nine

Honey chile',
sometimes I makes a big mess of things
but don't you see I got angel wings?
Angels lookin' out fer' me
when I ain't got sense enough
to be good company

Miss May carried the second batch of tarts into the dining room. But she was still too early. The old man living in the gray box up the hill wasn't nowhere to be seen, so she mopped the linoleum floors and stirred the big, banged up tin pot of pinto beans bubbling in the kitchen, then turned the fire off under them. Big Otis didn't say a word to anything she did.

Miss May found herself alone in the kitchen, with the pinto beans already stirred and the fire turned off. She sighed, feeling a mixture of frustration and embarrassment at her own behavior. Quickly, she carried a white plastic chair out the back door and settled into it, allowing herself a short nap in the misty rain.

Big Otis kept an eye on her through the little window in the backdoor. He watched her set the chair down on a slab of busted cee-ment and settled down into it like she was getting ready for the last call. Her snores roared right through the closed back door.

She finally woke up. She looked at her old, thin wristwatch. Lordy! It was almost two o'clock.

"Land's sakes!" she muttered, jumping up. Panicked by the time, she rushed back into the kitchen. Big Otis was talking to someone in the dining room. Assuming it couldn't be the peach-man, she hurried into the bathroom to compose herself. She combed her hands through her hair, grabbed paper towels and wiped her tunic top down.

But as she started to leave the tiny excuse for a bathroom, she was overcome with anger at her own foolishness. It was hopeless! She was going home!

She jerked the bathroom door open and made a run for the back door of the kitchen. As she made her dash for the back door, she was suddenly lifted off her feet. A big arm grabbed her around her middle, picked her up like she was an itty bitty feather, and carried her into the dining room. Shocked and mortified, she stammered incoherently while Big Otis sat her down in a chair.

Finally, she looked where Big Otis's finger was pointing. Yes. The peach-man had indeed returned! Big Otis walked over to the man. They turned their backs to her and started talking baseball, not missing a beat.

Big Otis stayed engrossed in conversation with the peach-man about baseball while Miss May smoothed her hair and settled her clothes until they were neat again. She was presentable now. She waited.

But the men still kept talking about baseball. She glared at them and grudgingly acknowledged their good manners.

Yet she couldn't help feeling irritated by their lack of interest in her. She was there. Hello! But the men kept on talking about baseball like it was the Holy Grail. Why, those foolish men were more interested in baseball than in tarts! But she was here to do business! Resigning herself to giving them one more chance, she interrupted their conversation to remind them of the business at hand.

"I hate to interrupt you men, but there is bidness' to be done here. Not to mention the beans might burn, and them ribs outside on the bar-b-q grill might need tendin'."

Big Otis started for the kitchen. She interrupted him.

"I'll stir them beans. Ya' best git' out there and turn them ribs."

Big Otis grabbed a pair of tongs and rushed out the front door.

Miss May leaned back in her chair and stared at the man. Her dress was dry again, and her mind was back in order.

Finally, the peach-man asked, "Aren't you going to stir the beans?"

She drawled, "Don't hafta'. Stirred and shut em' off 'fore I got hauled out here."

The peach-man blushed.

She stood and went to the kitchen. The peach-man sat down at the table and waited. While he waited, he tried to think about his island home, his family, and his world travels. Venice. That's good. Let me remember Venice. He begged his mind to relent, but it wouldn't.

Between the sharp rise in his newly found testosterone-"Good Lord," he murmured to himself.

"You've survived wars, old man... and now a woman you've just met is trying to make you mind-a woman with faded blue eyes, a too sharp, bossy little chin, that makes tarts an angel would covet."

Chapter Ten

Peach-man and Miss May
Gittin' together this day
each standin' alone
gnawin' on old bones

Peach-man- Gabriel Jackson Davis, Davis to his friends, sat in the tiny dining room that smelled of beans and bar-b-q. His posture perfect and patient, he awaited Miss May's return from the kitchen. A retired military veteran hailing from a small island in the South Pacific, Davis bore the weight of two Purple Hearts and the solemn duty of protecting a general's wife, now he was part-time chauffeur for her disabled husband.

In most respects, Davis was a man of remarkable strength and resilience, forged by years of military service and personal struggles. Yet, there was one weakness that gnawed at his resolve—a profound love for food that he inherited from his mother. Despite his efforts to conceal this passion, last week, his carefully constructed life was abruptly disrupted by the allure of peach tarts.

Since then, thoughts of the odd, funny little woman who'd introduced him to her peach tarts had consumed him incessantly. Also, there existed between them an instant, undeniable chemistry, an unspoken connection that tugged at his consciousness relentlessly. In her eyes, he'd seen a reflection of his own struggles, a blend of enduring pain and resilient hope. It was a familiarity that stirred something deep within him, a reminder of the burdens he once carried as an obese young islander with seemingly dim prospects.

Davis hoped fervently that the magnetic pull was mutual, that she too felt the palpable tension that lingered between them.

As he waited, Davis couldn't shake the feeling that his encounter with the woman and her luscious, tangy, crusted with angel wings peach tarts would mark the beginning of a new chapter in his life, one filled with uncertainty, yet tinged with the possibility of profound connection and unexpected joy.

Davis sensed the woman had fought many battles. And lost them. Maybe won a few.

He was reminded of the countless wounded souls he had encountered throughout his life—each bearing scars, both seen and unseen, from battles fought on various fronts.

In the woman he sat waiting for, he recognized familiar wounds, the vulnerability shielded by a front of defensiveness and chatter. Though he knew little of her past or the trials she had endured, he sensed the echoes of pain in her demeanor, subtle yet unmistakable.

He was more than curious. He had to know what had happened to her. What battles had she fought> What losses had she taken? What victories had she won? Davis understood the importance of patience and empathy. He recognized that making a friend was a journey that unfolded at its own pace, and he resolved to afford her every opportunity to connect with him.

With a silent vow to stand by her side, offering support and understanding, Davis waited, his commitment unwavering. In the quiet of the moment, he realized that their paths had converged for a reason, and he was determined to see it through, whatever the future might hold.

His thoughts were interrupted by the clanging of pots and pans in the kitchen. He grinned to himself and waited.

She returned, bearing trays laden with an array of tantalizing tarts. Davis's senses were immediately ensnared by the sweet aroma that filled the room. His eyes flitted between the sweet blackberry tarts and the bitter lemon tarts, uncertainty clouding his expression as he eyed the lemon tarts with suspicion.

He studied her. Her sharp little chin and her simmering ire. She studied him back. His clean, sharp profile. She frowned. He frowned. They both waited. Miss May planted her hands firmly on her hips. A defiant glint danced in her eyes.

"Them's my specialty," she declared proudly, pointing at the lemon tarts. "I call 'em Lemon Zingers. Some folks reckon they'll strip the hair right off your scalp. If you can handle 'em, then you can handle me. And if you can, well, I reckon you've earned yourself my name."

Her words hung in the air, charged with a mixture of challenge and invitation. Davis felt a surge of excitement mingled with apprehension as he regarded the Lemon Zingers before him. She was testing both his palate and his mettle, a symbolic, bakers gesture that hinted at the possibility of something deeper, something more meaningful than a mere exchange of names.

His eyes met hers with quiet determination.

She grinned as he reached out a cautious hand and plucked a lemon zinger out of its pan. He looked the tiny tart over, then sniffed it. His eyes widened. She watched as he pulled out a snow white handkerchief and mopped his face. He put his handkerchief away, popped the lemon zinger in his mouth, chewed and swallowed.

He coughed, then caught his breath. A look of delight swept over his face. He reached out a quick hand and plucked another lemon zinger out of its resting place and popped it into his mouth without hesitation. He chewed, swallowed then mopped his face again. Sweating profusely, he stared at her and grinned, waiting.

She gusted out a long sigh of acceptance. Bitterly she stated. "You win."

She stared down at the ancient linoleum, worn down to the wood beneath it in the spots where countless shoes and mops had scrubbed across the surface. Eyes still downcast, she blushed.

"My name is Miss May. I'm the daughter of that no good varmint John Elder and the long-sufferin', puttin' up with that same skunk, my mother Mz. Mona Jenkins, both of Callas, South Ka-lina."

She looked at him. They stared at each other. Despite their initial reservations, they couldn't deny the connection that was forming between them.

They both recognized what they were. Both older and wounded by life. Both lonely and guarded. Never getting too close to a sweetheart. Others, but no sweethearts allowed. Miss May felt comforted by Davis's presence, as if he were a safe harbor in the storm of her tumultuous life. And Davis, who had seen his fair share of battles, felt a sense of purpose at last.

"You're a long way from home." Davis finally stated, avoiding comment on the rest of her family history.

"So's Big Otis!" she retorted defensively. "He's from Atlanta."

He lifted his hands in surrender.

"Yes, ma'am," he said.

He quickly volunteered, "My name is Davis. Gabriel Jackson Davis of the Morgan Davis's, originally of the southern island of Saint Beautide, currently of New York City."

She cocked her head and looked at him curiously. "You're named after the Angel Gabriel?"

He blushed.

"Mothers with three daughters and only one son. What can you do? People who are wise call me by my last name, Davis."

He smiled at her.

She suddenly felt all settled back into herself.

"Well, Davis, we got some bidness' to take care of," she said.

In the midst of their tense exchange, a silent understanding began to take root between Miss May and Davis, despite the sharp edges of their words and the friction that crackled in the air.

Miss May, with her sharp tongue and unwavering independence, was inexplicably drawn to Davis's calm demeanor and quiet strength. His military background spoke of discipline and resolve, qualities that resonated deeply with her own sense of determination. Similarly, Davis found himself increasingly captivated by Miss May's resilience and fiery spirit. Her tenacity in the face of adversity stirred a growing admiration within him, tempered by recognition of the battles she must have fought and the scars she must bear from those battles.

Understanding and respect deepened between them. With a shared glance and a subtle nod, they acknowledged the unspoken truths lingering between them. In that moment, they spontaneously rubbed their hands together in anticipation of the challenges ahead. Each one knew that they were embarking on a journey that would test their limits and redefine their life.

Miss May sat down at the dining room table across form Davis.

"I would be delighted to conduct business with you, ma'am."

"Stop talkin' lak' a big shot." She ordered.

"Then may I call you Miss May?"

Her gaze fixed unwaveringly on him, Miss May pondered her next move with deliberate intent. Every word spoken and every action taken would shape the course of their relationship, determining the path they would tread together.

She stared at him, mulling it over. Whatever she decided, was gonna' set the way they moved forward. They both knew it. In that charged moment, both she and Davis knew that their conversation was at a pivotal juncture, a crossroads where the choices made could make or break their budding relationship.

With a sudden shift in her expression, a flicker of determination igniting in her flaming blue eyes, Miss May made her decision. She would lay the first piece of the foundation of the trust and respect they sought to cultivate between them. She would embrace the uncertainties that lay ahead.

"Well, if I'm gonna' call you Davis, then you best call me Miss May. Miss May is a good name. Suits me," she said resentfully, lower lip stuck out.

He studied her.

"Yes, yes it does suit you best. I'm going to call you Miss May."

She frowned. "At least for now," he hastily amended. "We shall become less formal as we get to know each other."

She stared at him and blushed again. She scrubbed a hasty hand across her hot, sweaty face.

Damn hormones! They were gonna' git' to know each other?

She stared down at her hands as though they were the only things in the world.

"I want it understood that this is strictly a bakin' bidness' relationship," she said without looking at him.

Her words hung heavy in the air. Davis felt the sting of them. She'd made a declaration tinged with defiance. She'd set a mean, limited boundary on their growing relationship.

They both knew it.

Davis, caught off guard by the meanness of her statement, felt a rush of angry warmth as he absorbed her words.

At last he realized that she was terrified. Finally, with a nod of inner understanding, he met her gaze with unwavering sincerity.

"Of course," he replied, his voice steady and calm, cool despite the turmoil swirling within him. "We can begin with the baking business, as you wish."

Davis hesitated, then blushed and stated again with determination, "We can definitely start there. Shall we discuss the baking business, then?"

Their eyes locked. Their professional arrangement wouldn't ever be enough. They both knew it. The unspoken words hung heavy in the air.

Davis. Just Davis. His name was Davis. He was causin' her to feel things. Like comforted. Like she was plumb wore out from an old illness an' he was a place to rest. Like his presence might give her strength to git' past the ol' stuff that kept a hold of her.

She'd tried pushin' on him, but he smoothed around her like water runnin' around a rock. She gritted her teeth. She'd tried to fight him but so far, it wasn't workin'. She glanced at him and realized that he knew she was fighting him and herself.

He was Davis. Just Davis. As they embarked on their journey together, Davis knew that this was going to be more than just a business partnership.

But for now, he would be a pillar of support. He hoped to eventually become a steadfast presence in her life, offering solace and strength in equal measure.

As they delved into the intricacies of their new baking business, Davis knew that even now, they were becoming each other's refuge in a world fraught with challenges and uncertainties.

Chapter Eleven

Tasty, tender lip smackin' rib love
Lemon zingers terrible tart sweet love
Blackberry tart purple sweet love
What else is there?
Nothin'. Ain't nothin'
Not a damn thing.

"How much do you charge for each lemon zinger tart, and how much for each blackberry tart? Or do you wish to sell them by the half or full dozen? And, will you be making more of the former peach tarts? They were memorable." Davis asked, as he smiled and drew a notebook and pen out of his pocket.

"Today is my day off this week. It changes with my employer's needs."

Miss May lowered her eyes.

"The price of everything keeps on goin' up. It ain't right, but it keeps on goin' up anyways.

Out of the blue Miss May announced sullenly, "You caused me some sufferin' last week."

Davis stared at her in surprise as she retrieved her odd looking orange purse from beside the stacked tart pans on the thin, rickety side table. She sat back down. He watched as she searched through the orange leather thing and finally drew out a fisted hand. She reached her closed fist slowly across the table towards him.

He watched in astonishment as she opened her fist. There lay the folded hundred dollar bill he'd laid on the table for her last week. She lay the money down in front of him.

"Take it," she ordered.

He stared at her, beginning to get a glimmer of how things were going to go in future dealings with Miss May.

He took the money and placed it by his hand. "Miss May, thank you," he said with a carefully blank face.

As he spoke, Davis's resolve hardened, his determination to assert his own reasonable boundaries growing stronger with each passing moment. He knew that compromise was essential in any partnership, but he refused to allow himself to be manipulated or exploited by anyone. Even Miss May.

She didn't know it yet, but she wasn't going to own every part of him. Nobody ever had, and nobody ever would. He knew people assumed that his good manners and mild surface would let them run all over him. His stubbornness began to build.

"Now, we can do bidness'," she said to him with satisfaction.

"I had to go berry pickin' three times in one week when I allus' jist' go once! An' then that wasn't enough. I had to make the lemon zingers 'cause I was so damn mad, and I needed them to bring the money up to the one hundred dollars you now owe me," she complained sullenly, gesturing to the stacks of tarts sitting neatly on the side table.

As Miss May voiced her grievances, Davis listened attentively, his demeanor calm yet resolute. While her words carried a hint of frustration, he couldn't help but detect a underlying sense of pride in her accomplishments.

With a subtle shift in his stance, Davis made it clear that he was no pushover, that beneath his mild exterior lay a steely resolve that brooked no disrespect. Though he respected Miss May's tenacity and determination, he was unwilling to be taken advantage of.

"I understand," he replied evenly, his tone firm yet respectful. "And I appreciate your dedication to your business. However, it's important to remember our agreement. The terms were clear from the outset."

He stared at her a minute. Then he slowly pushed the hundred-dollar bill back across the table.

Then he stood and crossed to the tart pans. He plucked out a lemon zinger and popped it in his mouth. Then he ate a blackberry tart. She glared at him, needing to scold him fer 'eatin' right out of the pans, and both of them knowin' it.

Miss May decided to leave well enough alone. After all, they was his tarts now. He could do what he wanted with 'em. She looked around.

Where the hell was Big Otis? He'd been gone too long. He oughta' be around when she was at his bar-b-q place without a smidgen of a thought of what she should do next. She sighed and stood.

"I'll get containers to put the tarts in, but you hafta' return 'em. They ain't free."

"I will return them to you," Davis answered her solemnly, eyeballing her as though he was standin' in front of a preacher takin' a marriage vow.

She loved the way he was looking at her! Miss May felt her heart soar at the sight of Davis's gaze. A rush of emotions overwhelmed her. With each step she took towards the kitchen, she felt the longing for him grow. It had been simmering beneath the surface for far too long.

She took two lingering steps toward the kitchen where the Tupperware lay in jumbled stacks at the end of the counter by the door.

"Davis," she shot him a blue fire look over her shoulder and sighed with longing that had grown bigger all her days. She couldn't stop herself.

"Davis," she called out again, her voice tinged with a mixture of desire and vulnerability, unable to contain the longing consuming her.

In response, Davis leapt to his feet. His own emotions were laid bare as he closed the distance between them in two swift strides. And then, in an instant, she found herself enveloped in his embrace, the warmth of his presence washing over her like a comforting embrace.

"Miss May!" he sighed.

"Miss May," he murmured again, his voice filled with a mixture of relief and tenderness, as if he had been waiting for this moment as eagerly as she had.

As they stood locked in each other's arms, Miss May felt a sense of completeness wash over her—a feeling that transcended words and defied explanation.

As they held each other close, she couldn't help but feel hope flicker to life within her. A hope that maybe, this moment marked the beginning of a long term love between them.

She turned her face up to be kissed like she used to when her granny was still alive, back when she was still a hopeful little girl about life.

Davis kissed her all right. He took the opportunity and made the most of it. She held on to him like a drowning person grabbing onto a life raft.

After a while she thought, I'm a clingin' to Davis like some kind of super glue or Velcro™, jist' the way Lucy Dotten clung to Junior Weathers out by the clothesline when she was a' hangin' up them white sheets and they both thought nobody could see 'em! Now I know why she did it, and never owned one hour of repentance over it!

Out loud she groaned, "I hope sweet baby Jesus ain't watchin' me right now, but knowin' him the way I do, he probably is." Desperately she cried out. "Lord help me!'

Davis murmured in her ear. "Shhh. It's okay."

With horror, she realized she'd spoken out loud. She tried to jerk away from Davis, but she ended up only bein' able to peel herself away from him a little bit at a time.

"Jist' like that damn Velcro™ stuff to take forever," she muttered.

She stepped back, smoothed her best tunic down and patted her hair back into place. She glanced around to see if Big Otis or anybody else had seen them smoochin'. The dining room was empty as a tomb. Well, it was still early. Big Otis was nowhere to be seen, not hoverin' around like a dam' disapprovin' fly, like always.

"Wise man," she muttered.

She fixed her attention on Davis, who was standing rooted to the faded linoleum floor, blushing like a new bloomed rose. She looked at the demure smile of contentment wreathing his mouth and frowned. She could easily guess what that man was thinkin'. She pointed a finger at him.

"I'll let you off the hook this time, but you better not try that again. I'm a lady, an' there ain't gonna' be no traffickin' around my good reputation!"

Davis blinked, momentarily taken aback by Miss May's stern admonition. Her sudden shift in demeanor caught him off guard, reminding him of the complexity of her character—a mixture of strength, pride, and a fierce determination to uphold her reputation.

Before he could speak, she scolded, "Now that your minute of foolishness is over, the one that I let you git' away with out of the kindness of my heart, I'm gittin' that Tupperware out of the kitchen like I started out to do."

He had allowed his emotions to get the better of him, forgetting for a moment the importance of maintaining her version of propriety and respect in their interactions.

He resolved to tread more cautiously in the future, to stay mindful of the boundaries that Miss May approved of.

Chapter Twelve

Love can be a tricky thing
involving tarts, Tupperware, or ring.
But sometimes, a little shove
is a necessary thing
Ever' body knows that!

Big Otis ran out the back door and closed it behind him before Miss May arrived in the kitchen. A big grin wreathed his face. He strolled around the side of the house and back in the front door, humming just like he'd been working outside the whole time, and never saw nothin'.

Miss May returned to the dining room, carrying a giant stack of Tupperware. She rolled her eyes at Big Otis who was leaning against the wall by a bowl of turnip greens, arms crossed, humming, a big grin on his face.

"Best you know right now which side your bread is buttered on, Mister."

"Oh, yeah, Miss May. I knows that fo' sure," Big Otis said, grinning and vanishing into the kitchen.

"Men!" Miss May said testily.

Davis watched her. He didn't answer. After the tarts were packed up and the one-hundred-dollar bill was earned, Davis watched her place the one-hundred-dollar bill carefully someplace in that odd looking pumpkin-size thing before she sat down at the table again. She stared at Davis and waited. He sat down, cleared his throat, and spoke in a formal voice.

"I would like to continue to purchase your wares. What will you have available next Monday?"

She glared at him.

"Monday? What happened to Wednesdays? That only gives me five days to git' somethin' ready," she complained.

"Like I said earlier, Miss May, sometimes my days off change."

"I dis-remembered that 'til jist now," she answered sullenly. He waited while she mulled it over.

Finally, she snuck a hot, blushing look at him and said, "I don't know 'bout changin' the schedule. You best be behavin' from now on?"

She looked horrified as she realized her scoldy words sounded like a question. Davis looked properly crestfallen.

"I've learned my lesson, Miss May. It won't happen again like that." Davis spread his hands out, palms up. "But it couldn't, anyway, could it?" he grinned.

"If'n you's gonna' joke lak' that, I'm done witcha!" Miss May protested and jumped to her feet. Miss May was having none of it. Her protestations rang out, her resolve unwavering as she jumped to her feet, eyes flashing with defiance.

Davis rose to his feet as well. The air thickened with unspoken words and unresolved emotions. It was a standoff.

Davis finally broke the stalemate, his actions speaking louder than words as he collected the bags of tarts from the side table. With a terse nod, he made his way towards the front door, the weight of Miss May's parting words lingering in the air.

"See you Monday," he said, tossing the words over his shoulder as he went out the front door.

"Not if I see you first!" she retorted.

For a moment, Davis froze, the realization dawning upon him that Miss May would always need to have the last word—a fact that he would have to come to terms with if their budding relationship was to stand a chance.

With a resigned shrug, he turned towards her one last time, his gaze softening with understanding. "At two o'clock," he affirmed, before stepping out into the fading light of the evening, leaving behind the echoes of their tumultuous encounter and the promise of a new beginning.

She cried that night. Great big, loud, mad bawlin'. She was scared to death of what was happening. Of the kissin'. Of how much she liked it. Of Davis. She'd been down that road before. And ever' time, she'd lost her baking skills for awhile.

The baking problem started back when she was seven and baked the mornin' biscuits black three times on purpose before they turned her out of the house to cool off.

She'd lingered on the porch and slept in the lean-to with the cow until she got over bein' mad at 'em. It took a few days until she got real hungry. That's how strong her mad was.

She'd picked dewberries and currants in a bucket and stewed them in clean water until they was bustin' open. Then she'd run up on the porch and set 'em against the door until they called her in to cook 'em. That was the first time. There was more times, more times at the home place, the rest happened in other places.

She stayed skinny with a big belly from starvin' too many times as a young un'. Now she'd put on age weight and was shaped like one of them gut heavy oat farmers out Sizemore Way. Still little and mad, she wore stretch pants and loose, long tops from the thrift store.

She cried that night, tryin' to drown out the flame of hope blazin' in her that had held its face up to be kissed by Davis.

"Damn traitor!" she shouted. "Die!"

"You'll jist' git' hurt again!"

"Don't you remember a damn thing?"
But the hopeful part of her that mooned over romance magazines and old black and white

movies, stuck like that stubborn Velcro™ to its hope. It gave her pert, smartass answers.

"But what if it turns out okay?"

"But what if he likes us?"

"Mmm mmm! That kiss was good as sugar candy!"

"Bet he wants to kiss us again."

"Monday's a' comin'. Full force. Four days from now. An' we gotta' have somethin' special ready fer' that man."

Her innards argued back and forth until she fell into a dead sleep from exhaustion.

Miss May left early to go blackberry pickin' in the rain the next morning. The weather suited her dark mood. She carried plastic containers to put the soggy berries in. She didn't give a damn that she looked like a homeless old woman to the city people. Ever' body better leave her be. She hurried along like she had a place to go to, so people would leave her alone and not call somebody on her, like she was a lost old person. She'd like awful much to whip somebody's ass, but nobody else was out in the rain. She relaxed and let the rain soak her good. She took her umbrella to make it look like she was in her right mind, though. She picked a few berries, but it was too dam' wet. Yep. It felt good to get out of the house. After awhile she wandered home, a wet, rebellious vagrant, dried off, ate and went to sleep again. When she woke up, she muttered, "Damn men!" She got up and looked out the window. The rain had stopped.

The days fled by. Monday showed up like it was in a big dam' hurry to git' there.

"Gonna' be a tough day," she nodded grimly to herself, sneezin' over and over.

Big Otis' wares was due ever' Wednesday. But she baked the blackberry tarts early for him 'cause he'd not uttered one word of complaint about havin' to go without her deluxe dessert wares. She used saved back freezer berries to make 'em.

Chapter thirteen

Smarty Pants and Dancing
Swords of Words
don't git' too callous now!
...or Leavin' joins the game
as an unwelcome guest

Davis arrived much too early. He watched from the parking lot as Big Otis rescued an old man who'd pissed himself and could barely walk. He watched Big Otis carry the little old man up the street and settle him into a white plastic chair in front of the OK Corral Bar-b-q. Big Otis wiped him down, then went inside, came back out and set a rib plate on his lap, then went inside again.

After Big Otis was back inside, Davis strolled over to the patio, grabbed a plastic chair and set it close to the old man. He settled himself into it and waited. The old man didn't pay any attention to Davis, he just chewed on his rib.

"Where do you live?" Davis finally asked him. "Are you related to Big Otis?"

The old man stopped chewing on the rib and dropped it on his plate. He lowered his head in shame.

"I pissed all over myself again. I ain't got no more clean pants to piss now," he complained. He pointed up the hill at the tall gray warehouse for old people. "I live up there. They won't keep my laundry done up."

The old man picked up his rib again.

Davis looked the old man over, then he stood up and looked at his watch. It was too early to meet Miss May. He went down the sidewalk and into the giant pharmacy. In a few minutes, he came out carrying two bags. He strolled back up the sidewalk, set the bags down by the old man, and sat down again.

The old man kept chewing his rib.

"What ya' got there?" Big Otis asked, coming outside to stoke the bar-b-q grill.

"You's here mighty early."

"Yes," Davis admitted, shamefaced.

"Too early."

Big Otis grinned.

Davis said, "In the meantime, though, I have made the acquaintance of this elderly gentleman. Would you happen to know his name?"

"It's Baird. Lenny Baird of the Coconut Bairds. He's got a 'partment in that sorry excuse for an old folks place."

Big Otis pointed up the hill to the ugly, gray utility box towering over the block.

"That's why they built that pharmacy down there," he said, motioning down the hill, "to keep 'em drugged. Lenny needs a little help sometimes gittin' back up the hill to home. His meds, ya' know. He has to have 'em."

Lenny watched them, listening.

"You want a cola?" Big Otis said.

Davis and Lenny nodded.

"I'm gonna' git' us some. I'll be right back."

He disappeared. Davis placed another white plastic chair beside his and Lenny's. Big Otis came back out, handed three colas around, then set down. They all took a long drink.

Lenny sucked noisily on his straw, then asked, "Wanna' tell me what's in them sacks?"

Davis grinned. He reached into the bigger sack and brought out three pairs of pants. Navy blue, black and dark brown. He plucked Lenny's plate from his lap and placed it carefully on a nearby table. Then he laid the new pants on Lenny's lap. Lenny ran his fingers over them and grinned.

"Hot dog!" he whispered hoarsely.

"Well, I never thought of doin' that... What's in the other sack?" Big Otis asked.

"Well," Davis said, blushing.

"It's a man's secret. Us men have special needs sometimes. Sometimes we need things that protect both our dignity and our sorry assets!"

He reached in and pulled out a large pack of adult incontinence underwear. Lenny grabbed at them like a drowning man. Tears ran down his cheeks.

"I haven't had any of these in a long time

Big Otis, astounded, said, "You should have told me, Lenny."

Lenny peered up at him. "Told you what?"

Big Otis just shook his head.

He turned to Davis.

"Well, hell, if' I'd thought about it...damn glad YOU did."

Big Otis grabbed up Lenny's plate, grabbed the pants and underwear off Lenny's lap with one big paw, and slapped the plate back down on it. He handed the things to Davis, who put the items back in the bags. Big Otis sat back down in his chair. He and Davis didn't look at each other.

"Think it's gonna' rain?" Big Otis asked.

All three of them look up at the clear sky.

"Maybe."

Lenny went back to gnawing on his rib. Big Otis and Davis shaded their eyes and talked about the weather. They talked until Lenny finished his rib and started to nod off. They threw his paper plate away and wiped him down while he dozed.

Big Otis picked him up in his arms like he was a little feather. Davis grabbed Lenny's walker and the pharmacy bags. Big Otis carried Lenny up to his apartment in the gray utility box and tucked him into his recliner. Davis placed the two pharmacy bags in Lenny's arms.

Lenny woke up long enough to smile and clutch the two bags close to his chest before he nodded off again.

"The coconut Bairds are all Cookoo." he said before drifting off to sleep.

Big Otis and Davis strolled back down the hill to the Ok Corral Bar-b-q.

Big Otis rolled his eyes at Davis. "You might wanna' make yourself scarce til' she gits' here."

They both knew who he meant.

Davis nodded and said, "I shall return promptly at two."

Chapter fourteen

Better late than never
Dat's what they say
When de' 'ol folks
Come out to play
Ha ha!

It was Monday. Miss May's eyes opened. Her heart fluttered like a bird caught in a net. She was scared to death of what was happenin'. She gritted her teeth. Too dam' bad. She was doin' it anyways. No more runnin'. She was too damn old. She was tired of bein' a bored, chicken shit, moron, hormonal, lonesome old dipstick.

"Well, Hell's on its way agin'. Doan' wanna' stand in its way and git' mowed down agin'."

Trouble was looming on the horizon.

"Bidness' attire," she thought awhile later, patting her hair into place in front of the small wavy mirror tacked on the back of the bathroom door.

"What the hell you got to lose anyway? Ain't no phone calls comin' in. Ain't no family comin' 'round. Nobody to help you or to live with."

She nodded sagely at her image in the mirror.

"An' you ain't a' gittin' no younger, either," she said accusingly, pointing a finger, frowning and muttering at the mirror.

Miss May was resigned to her fate, but also determined to make a change, even if it meant confronting some unpleasant truths. Miss May's eternal sense of isolation and desperation was underscored by the realization that there was little left for her in her current situation. So why not take a chance?

Miss May kept grappling with the unexpected circumstances and gearing up for a showdown, both figuratively and perhaps literally.

"Ain't nothin' left 'cept Big Otis and his place. The OK Corral Bar-b-q. An' dat ain't enough if I can git' me more. Dat' was enough before, but no mo'. Damn changes! Goin' back there to see that man agin'."

She grinned. However, that man and Big Otis was gonna' git' a surprise today.

She smoothed down the purple tunic with the big red flowers that matched best with her newest stretchy pants. The red floral tunic came off of the dummy down at Claude's Thrift Shop. It cost fifty cents. She had chosen the purple tunic with big red flowers to deliberately add a touch of eccentricity and personality to her character. She wasn't afraid to stand out, even in this big rainy, drab dressing city!

She studied her worn out pink sneakers.
"Not yet!" she muttered. Why did people want you to git' rid of all the things you liked the best? She refused to conform to others' standards of what she should or shouldn't like or keep. Miss

May was determined to hold onto the things that brought her joy, regardless of their perceived value by others. She lifted the brown grocery bag full of tart trays, and settled it carefully into the wicker baby buggy.

Claude the Thrift Man had sold the buggy to her. 'Ol Claude was a ninety year old charmer, white headed, thin as a toothpick, sharp as a tack. Claude liked her cornbread. Yep. She'd taken him a batch of honey cornbread and it worked like magic, since she'd already planned on getting some improvements for herself and her baking bidness' out of his place for a good price.

When she was ready, she rolled the buggy out the door. Up, up, she went, headin' towards Big Otis's Bar-b-q, pushing the buggy in front of her.

She stopped and sat down on the curb and retied her sneakers. She fanned herself and spoke to no one there.

"I'll hafta' grease dem' dam' wheels," she complained to nobody there.

Davis arrived at the OK Corral Bar-b-q promptly at two. He strolled into the little dining room as though he was just passin' by.

Miss May was sitting at the table, a yellow number # 2 pencil and a notepad by one hand. Davis glanced at the tarts stacked neatly in Tupperware containers on the rickety side-table.

There were more of them than he'd anticipated. He looked around. That damn Big Otis was nowhere in sight. He heard clanging in the kitchen. Resigned to his fate, Davis frowned. He sat down in the chair across from Miss May and waited.

She picked up the pencil and slid the notepad in front of her. Head down, she jotted notes. After awhile she spoke.

"So now I got two clients to supply, an' I kin' only do so much! The point a' this here bidness' meetin' is for you and Big Otis..."

She looked toward the kitchen and shouted his name. Quickly Big Otis stepped into the tiny, hot dining room, his forehead beaded with sweat.

Davis's large, dark eyes sparkled with approval. This little woman wasn't afraid of that mountain of a man who'd beat the hell out of countless boxing men back in the day! Davis glanced at Big Otis' huge ham-fisted hands. He could still twist a pot into a kettle if he wanted to, Davis decided.

Davis sat back and looked Miss May over. Purple with big red flowers. Her top reminded him of his island roots. He liked that. Well, Miss May owned her own kind of grit. He just needed to find out how far it went, and how it worked. He leaned farther back in his chair. Miss May pulled her glare off of Big Otis and fastened it on him. He straightened in his chair

She snapped, "It ain't right, but costs keeps on goin' up, anyways, so don't you go gittin' any ideas about overbookin' any more orders either!"

"What do you mean?" Davis asked.

She glared at him, frosty blue eyes shaded with a frown under lovely moth wing eyebrows. Davis felt a sudden urge to reach across the table and smooth the wings back into place, but wisely resisted the urge.

Her eyes softened. The frost fled. She mumbled, "Oh well," and looked down again. She blushed and began furiously adding numbers with the yellow pencil on the pad of paper. Davis studied her small, downturned mouth and sharp little nose with fascination.

Big Otis, forgotten by both of them, turned back to the kitchen, relieved at having been dismissed. He shot Davis a sympathetic look on his way out. Davis looked away from Miss May for a second and grinned back at him. Big Otis shook his head, turned his broad back to both of them, and danced off into the kitchen.

Miss May added numbers until her blush faded, then she looked up and shoved the notepad across the table to him.

"Like I said, it ain't right, but prices keeps on goin' up anyways." she snapped.

Davis picked up the penciled list and looked it over. He laid it down, and ran his long fingers through his neatly trimmed, short gray hair.

"Whew!' he said. He didn't know what else to say, for his attention had been arrested by the curve of Miss May's high cheekbones. A nervous tic appeared at the corner of his eye.

She stared at him in wonder, noticing his tic. Slowly she began understanding that he was nervous around her. Maybe he was interested in her, and not so much the tarts? She suddenly understood that she wasn't alone in her hope of companionship and maybe a better future. Davis might be standin' with her in it, too.

"Survivin's kept me from lookin' too close at anythin' much," she muttered to him in apology.

"Yes. It is that way for many," Davis answered, comforting her with his words. A silent moment of understanding passed between them. Davis reached his hand cautiously across the table. She let him hold her hand for a few seconds before she pulled it away.

"Would you consider dining with me soon, Miss May?" Davis asked.

She frowned. He could tell she was about to refuse. He sighed. He'd asked too soon.

"We could call it a business dinner." he wheedled.

She stared at him and finally said "Okay."

Chapter fifteen

I see's what's goin' on
Hain't got too far to go
Left their fingerprints behind
Ha!
Pairin' ain't parin'.
All it is,
is silly sharin'.

Big Otis was watching them through the wide crack in the crooked kitchen door. With his keen eye for matchmaking, he observed the connection building between Miss May and Davis. It had been awhile since he played Cupid. He listened to their last words. The words holding a dinner invitation. Why wait for a dinner date? Strike while the iron's hot! He would serve them delicious food right now! He had this Cupid thing down. He knew exactly what was needed. He would create an atmosphere that would promote their growing romance!

He grinned a huge, silent grin and went to humming a hymn from his childhood as he swung into action. Quick as a flash, he slapped ribs and sides and cornbread on two plates and rushed them out to the table where the two lovebirds sat, staring at each other. He slapped the full plates down in front of them.

"Samples. Try 'em. Paper towels on yore' left, bar-b-q sauce on your right, utensils and buttah' fer' da' bread comin' up!"

Before they could say a word, Big Otis danced back into the kitchen, humming real loud. In a few seconds, he returned and clattered down foiled butter pats and worn, tarnished forks.

"Doan' jist' set there! Start eatin'! Best start them dinner dates right here! Times a' wastin', and none of us are gittin' any younger! Besides, it looks like both of you need the practice!"

"I'll take mine to go!" Miss May replied smartly, for she liked his ribs better than honeycomb, and couldn't say no to them however they were offered.

Davis reached his hand across the table and touched her hand. She jerked her hand back, startled.

"Why don't we humor Big Otis? Just this once?" Davis persuaded in a gentle voice. Miss May frowned, swallowed her pride, nodded. Big Otis fled back to the kitchen.

Resentfully she said, "I'll do it 'cause I'm hungry. I ain't eat a bite this live long day 'cause a' you and him. You're both to fault."

Davis mulled over her words and nodded.

"You're absolutely right. We apologize. Thoroughly."

Big Otis peeked through the door crack again. Wisely, he stayed in the kitchen until they finished eating.

Davis lingered as long as he could before he left. Miss May carried their empty plates to the kitchen where Big Otis had cleaned everything three times over.

She looked around. "Cleanest I've ever seen this joint!" she stated tartly. She pointed her finger at him.

"Don't you ever do that to me agin'! Why, I had to eat with him jist' to keep from hurtin' a new clients feelin's!"

Big Otis grinned. "I'll do it agin' Miss May, ever' chance I gets!"

"You big ol' stubborn fool!" she shouted.

Big Otis stood his ground. He watched her anger fade into confusion and hope.

"Now I gotta' bring that peach-man tarts next week. He doan' know it, but he's gonna' git' more than he bargained for!"

"He shore is, Miss May!"

Big Otis responded fervently.

She frowned at him.

"I mean to bring him lemon zingers too!"

Big Otis knew what that meant. They'd reached a draw. Like in boxing. She knew it, too.

A long silence went on. Then Miss May said, "We're a' meetin' here next Wednesday. On account of bidness'. Two o'clock."

"That's good, Miss May," Big Otis said. "Wanna' help me fill some takeout orders? They'll be here to pick 'em up real soon. I put my customers off as long as I could so's you two lovebirds could sit a spell. An' can ye' turn the door sign 'round that says we're closed? Looks like we're open now!"

A rumble started deep in his big chest. Big Otis erupted with laughter. He laughed loud and long.

"Best fun I've had in a long time! Better than watchin' a world cham-peen' boxin' match!"

Miss May turned red. She huffed out of the kitchen.

"Men!"

The next week when they were to meet, Big Otis was better prepared. He admired Davis and liked Miss May, who was a piece of work. Yeah. He would help them out.

He propped the front door open. It was almost noon. He drew in a grateful sniff of the smoky rib smell curlin' up from the bar-b-q grill settin' big and tidy in the right corner of his refined patio.

"Thankee Lawd, for ever' thaing."

He drawled his words out loud and slow, lookin' right and left to see if any haints' had abided there durin' the night. Nothin'. Good. He yawned and strolled back inside. All was right with his world. Except somethin' kept naggin' at him.

He finally realized what was bothering him.

It was Davis and Miss May.

Big Otis had caught the matchmaking bug!
Why, he'd turned into a damn matchmaker,
stayin' awake at night tryin' to figure out more
ways to git' 'em together. He shook his head.
Losin' sleep over somebody else's love plot. He
was a damn fool! What the hell was the matter
with him?

Big ol' boxer-man loves love fools! he thought,
mincing across the faded linoleum, bar-b-q
tongs in one giant ham hand. Big Otis knew he
was their unexpected ally. He would help Davis
and Miss May's journey toward romance.
Companionship and a better future lay before
them, with his help. What other schemes might
he, Big Otis aka Cupid, cook up to bring them
together? He grinned and batted his eyes and
pursed a big smacky kiss into the air and waved
the tongs around.

"What the hell are you doing?" Miss May
snapped.

In a flash, he knew the next move needed to
shove along the little romance that was budding
at the Ok Corral Bar-b-q.

Big Otis stopped and put his hands on his
hips. He assessed Miss May with his eyes. He
nodded. Yep. She was small and desperate,
allus' needin' the last word, standin' there with
her sharp little chin a' quiverin'.
Oh well, he thought. With Miss May, it would
take a lot of shovin'. Maybe even a bulldozer. He
pictured her easily holding a bulldozer back with

one hand, making it mind her, its wheels spinning, her giving it hell. He grinned and wisely decided to keep his thoughts to himself, even though she'd startled him. Not a smart thing to do to a Cupid matchmaker. Caused him to make even more plans.

He glanced at the 1945 calendar hanging on a rusty nail on the wall. Large and grease stained, a picture of the Brown Bomber, Joe Louis, was above the twelve tiny calendars printed on the page below.

Davis would be coming in soon. Big Otis eyed the wicker buggy she was pulling.

"Whatcha' got in dere'?"

"Nevah' you min' jist yit.' I'll show you when..." she hesitated then scowled.

"HE git's here," Big Otis finished her sentence, grinned, nodded, and turned away.

Miss May pulled up a chair and arranged the buggy beside it. She smoothed her clothes and patted her hair into place before she turned the "Dine in or Dine Out" handwritten sign over. On the back the sign read: "Takeout only."

Davis stepped through the door just as Miss May turned the sign over.

"How are you today, Miss May?' he asked politely. "I've been looking forward to your lemon zingers."

"They's some right here. I made 'em jist' fer' you."

Davis took a step towards the table. Miss May warned him off with a quick hand.

"Doan' be a' thinkin' about samplin' any of my wares."

Davis froze in mid stride. He rolled his eyes at Big Otis, who in turn, rolled his eyes up to Heaven and started laughing. His laughter was Great and Big and hollow. Lots of room inside to step into. It was an invitation to sweep aside for a brief moment, the rigid yardsticks used to measure other people and their situations.

Soon, all three of them were laughing. Their laughter filled the OK Corral Bar-b-q and rolled out the door. People hurrying by on their prim, solemn, damp duties heard the laughter. Some of them grinned openly, others grinned secretly, others ignored the sound.

As the laughter subsided and the moment passed, Miss May and Davis found themselves drawn closer together, their bond strengthened by shared experience. Big Otis, ever the romantic at heart, smiled to himself, content in the knowledge that he had played his part in bringing the two souls together.

With a sense of fulfillment, Big Otis returned to his duties, leaving Miss May and Davis to continue on their journey of discovery and love. And as the laughter of their moment lingered in the air, the patrons of the OK Corral Bar-b-q couldn't help but smile, knowing that love had found its way into their midst.

And so, with laughter and love, another chapter closed at the OK Corral Bar-b-q, leaving behind a tale of unexpected connections and the magic of human kindness.